ENID BLYTON LIBRARY

Titles in this series

The Rude Little Rabbit
The Lucky Green Pea
The Pixies and the Primroses
The Tale of Scissors the Gnome

ISBN 0-86163-638-4

Text copyright © Darrell Waters Limited
Illustrations copyright © 1994 Award Publications Limited

Enid Blyton's signature is a trademark of Darrell Waters Limited

The Tale of Scissors the Gnome first published 1941
as Enid Blyton's Book of the Year by Evans
How Derry the Dormouse Lost His Secret first published 1951
as The Magic Snowbird by Pitkin
This edition first published 1994

Published by Award Publications Limited,
Goodyear House, 52-56 Osnaburgh Street, London NW1 3NS

Printed in Belgium

Enid Blyton

The Tale of Scissors the Gnome

&

How Derry the Dormouse
Lost his Secret

Illustrated by Rene Cloke

AWARD PUBLICATIONS LIMITED

There was once a tiny old man called Scissors. He was a gnome, and if you measure out six centimetres on your ruler, and cut out a little man that high, you will know just how small Scissors was!

He carried a pair of scissors about half as high as himself, and with them he cut out anything his friends wanted.

A snip of his scissors and
a coat would be cut out.
Another snip or two and a
party frock would be all ready
for sewing up. He was a
wonder with his scissors was
the old gnome.

There was just one thing he was afraid of and that was rather strange, for he was afraid of the rain. We love to feel the rain on our faces, but Scissors was terrified. One big drop of rain on his head and he would be knocked flat on the ground, for he was so small. Once a drop of rain had broken his arm and he hadn't been able to cut out clothes with his scissors for three months.

Raindrops were as big as dinner-plates to him! So you can guess that if it began to rain, Scissors would run for shelter at once. If ever he went out he took with him his green umbrella, which was ten centimetres round and covered him well.

And then one day, when he had gone
to visit the elf in the garden-bed,
somebody stole his umbrella.

He had put it down for one moment
whilst he cut out a pink dress and
somebody crept up behind him and ran
off with his precious umbrella!

Poor Scissors! No sooner did he miss his green umbrella than it began to rain! Plop! A drop fell on his head and sent him on his nose. Plop! One went on his back and took away all his breath. Plop! A third drop made him so wet that he looked as if he had been swimming for weeks.

"Help! Help! Lend me an umbrella, please!" yelled Scissors. But nobody was near except the elf whose dress he had been making. She was a scatterbrained little creature and didn't know what to do.

But nearby was a strong nasturtium plant, and the flowers called to Scissors. "Pick one of our flat leaves! They will shelter you well. They are just like flat umbrellas!"

So Scissors gratefully picked a leaf, held it by the stalk, and stood under it whilst the rain poured down. It made a wonderful umbrella, and Scissors was pleased.

"I'd like to do something for you, nasturtiums," he said, when the rainstorm was over. "What can I do? Do you want any dresses, coats or hats cut out to wear?"

"Of course not!" laughed the nasturtiums. "We already have orange and yellow dresses to wear. But you might cut us a pretty little fringe in the centre, Scissors – a nice whiskery one."

So the gnome took his scissors and cut a fine fringe in the middle of the flowers.

And if you don't believe me, go and look! As for his umbrella, Scissors never found it, but he always keeps a stock of nasturtium umbrellas in water, ready for when he goes out. Isn't he funny and wise too!

How Derry the Dormouse
Lost his Secret

Once upon a time Derry the
dormouse hid a nice little store of
cherry-stones in the hole of a hollow
tree. He was so pleased with them
that he went to look at them every
day. Sometimes he nibbled one, and
when he came to the kernel inside
he ate it all up.

But he couldn't keep his secret to himself. When he met Bright-Eyes the squirrel, he called to him:

"Bend your head down, Bright-Eyes, and I will tell you something. I have a store of cherry-stones in the hollow tree! It is nice to have a secret like that!"

Bright-Eyes listened, and then leapt up the trunk of a tree. At the top he found Screech the jay, looking very colourful in the sun.

"Bend your head down, Screech, and I will tell you something," he said. "Someone has a store of cherry-stones in the hollow tree. There is a secret for you if you like!"

Screech opened his beak and made a noise like his name. Then he flew off and came down in a field where Four-Paws the hare was nibbling grass.

"Bend your head down, Four-Paws, and I will tell you something," said Screech. "Someone has a store of cherrystones in the hollow tree. There is a secret for you if you like!"

Four-Paws listened eagerly and then went pounding over the field. It wasn't long before he met Mowdie the mole.

"Bend your head down, Mowdie, and I will tell you something," he said. "Someone has a store of cherry-stones in the hollow tree. There is a secret for you if you like!"

Mowdie listened and then ran off in a hurry. Soon she saw Grunt the hedgehog, and she spoke to him.

"Bend your head down, Grunt, and I will tell you something," she said. "Someone has a store of cherry-stones in the hollow tree. There is a secret for you if you like!"

Grunt listened, and then went on his way down the ditch. Soon he met Flicker the robin, and he called to him.

"Bend your head down, Flicker, and I will tell you something," he said. "Someone has a store of cherry-stones in the hollow tree. There is a secret for you if you like!"

Flicker listened and flew off. When he saw Fuff-Fuff the long-tailed fieldmouse, he called to him.

"Bend your head down, Fuff-Fuff, and I will tell you something," said Flicker. "Someone has a store of cherry-stones in the hollow tree. There is a secret for you if you like!"

Fuff-Fuff listened and ran off. He went straight to the hollow tree, and there he found the store of cherry-stones. Then, quickly and quietly, he carried them one by one in his mouth to where he had his home in a hole in the bank of the field.

That evening Screech, Four-Paws, Mowdie, Grunt and Flicker all met together with Derry, and with one accord they began to tell him his secret.

"Oh, Derry," they said. "We have a secret to tell you. Someone has a store of cherry-stones in the hollow tree."

"Why, that is my secret!" cried Derry the dormouse, in surprise. "How is it you all know it? But, since you do know it, come and I will show you my store of cherry-stones in the hollow tree."

He took them to the tree, and they all peered in. Alas, the hole was empty! No cherry-stones were to be seen at all.

"Oh! Oh!" wept Derry the dormouse. "Now my secret is gone. My cherry-stones are stolen. If I had only kept my secret, I would have kept my stones too! Where, oh where, is my little store of cherry-stones?" But no one knew. Only Fuff-Fuff could have told him, and he was sitting in his hole, nibbling through the cherry-stones to get at the kernels inside. Oh, naughty little Fuff-Fuff!